DC SUPER FRIENDS

WONDER WOMAN™
AN AMAZING HERO!

Written by Mary Tillworth

Illustrated by Erik Doescher

A GOLDEN BOOK • NEW YORK

All rights reserved. Published in the United States by Golden Books, an imprint of Random House Children's Books, a division of Penguin Random House LLC, 1745 Broadway, New York, NY 10019, and in Canada by Penguin Random House Canada Limited, Toronto. Golden Books, A Golden Book, A Big Golden Book, the G colophon, and the distinctive gold spine are registered trademarks of Penguin Random House LLC.

randomhousekids.com   ISBN 978-1-5247-1840-4 (trade) — ISBN 978-1-5247-1841-1 (ebook)   Printed in the United States of America

10 9 8 7 6 5 4 3 2

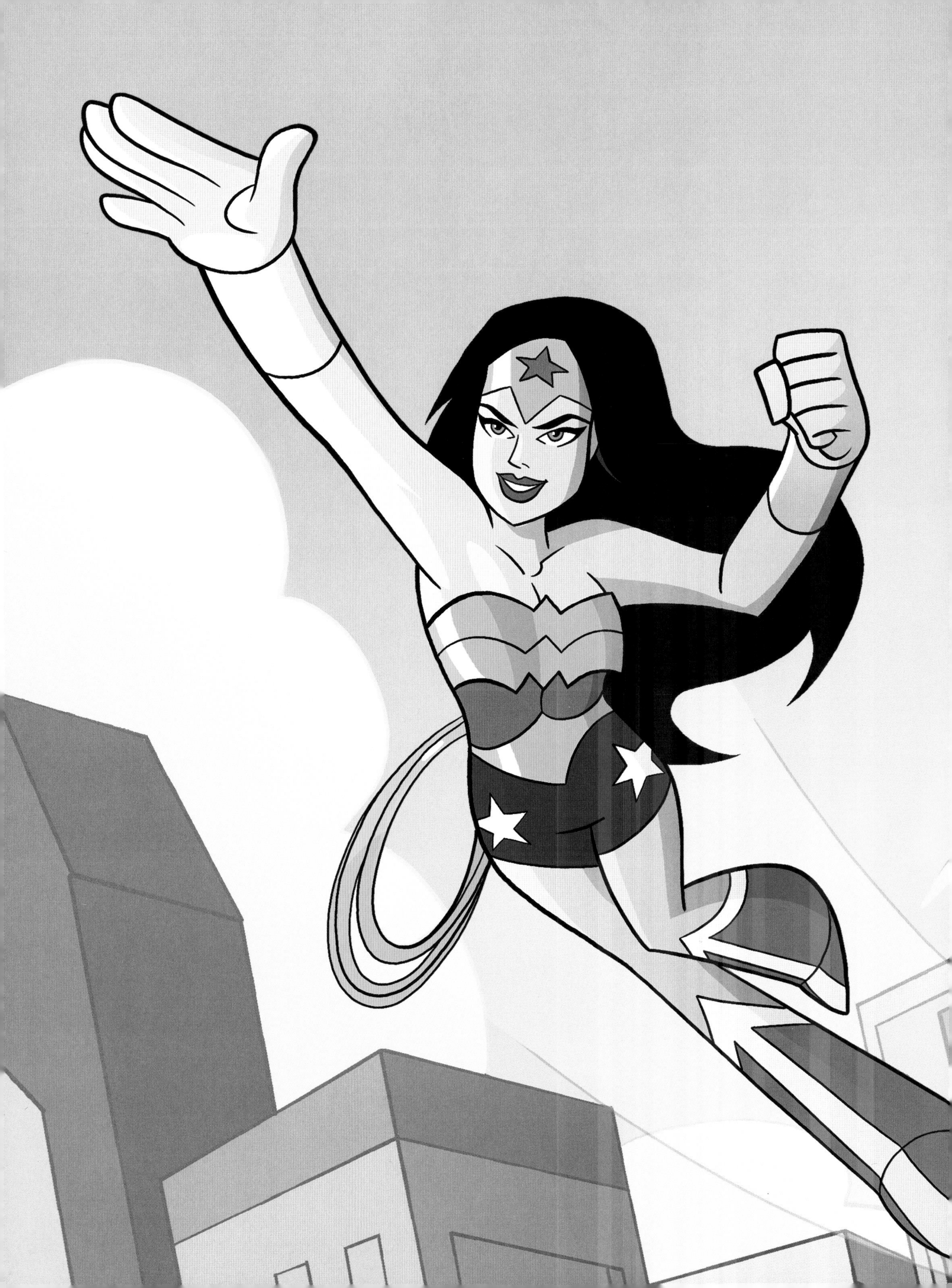

High above the clouds, a mighty super hero swoops through the sky. She is the guardian of the people, a warrior princess sworn to protect the innocent. She is **Wonder Woman!**

This amazing super hero has dedicated her life to eliminating evil from the world. With her incredible powers and skills, Wonder Woman is nearly unstoppable!

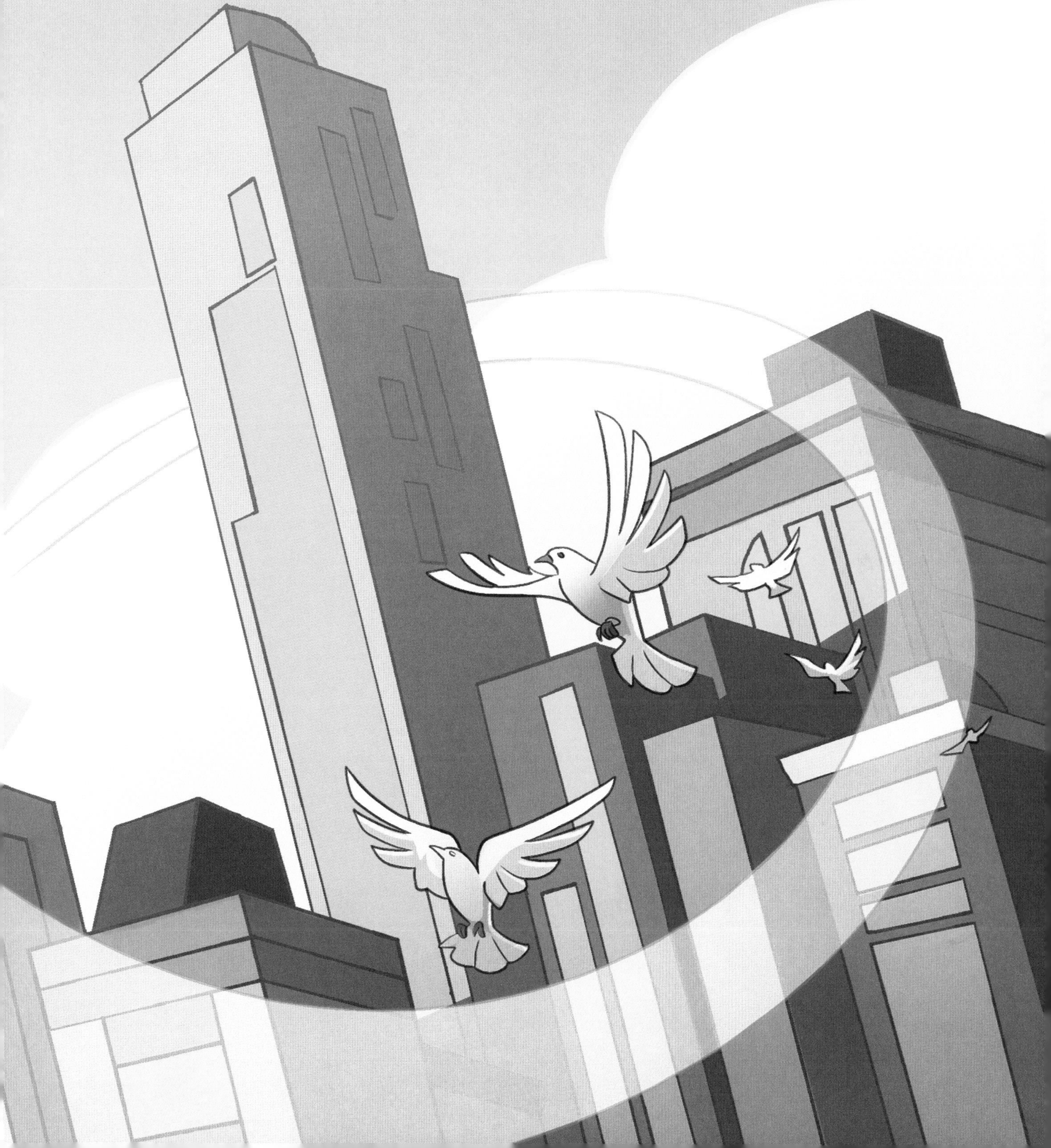

Wonder Woman was raised by a group of women called Amazons on the mysterious and secluded Paradise Island. Even as a young girl, Wonder Woman was very **fast** and **strong**.

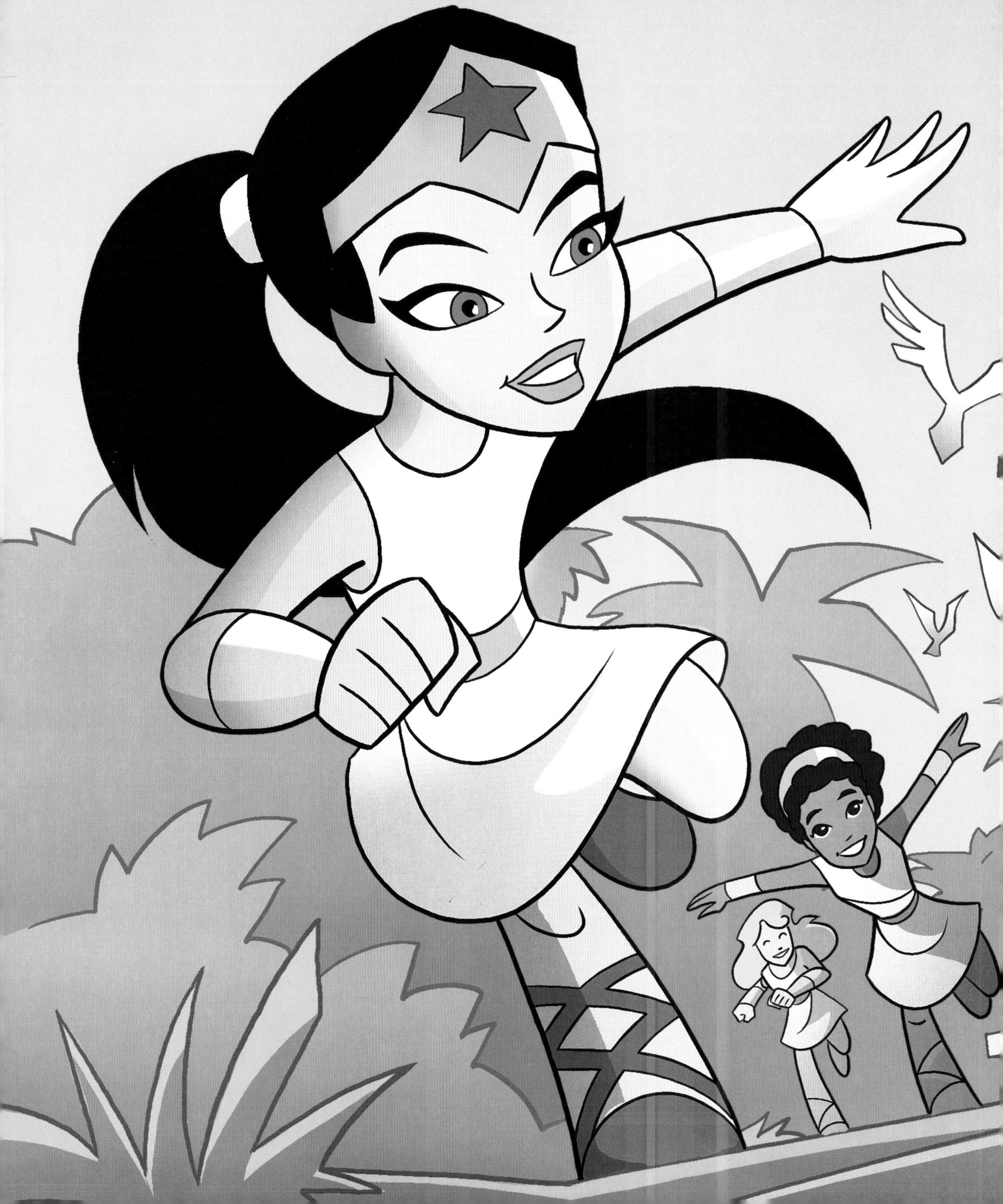

Wonder Woman's mother, Hippolyta, was Queen of the Amazons. Hippolyta was extremely proud of her daughter, Princess Diana. She taught her to be fierce and fearless, but also ***loving*** and ***kind***.

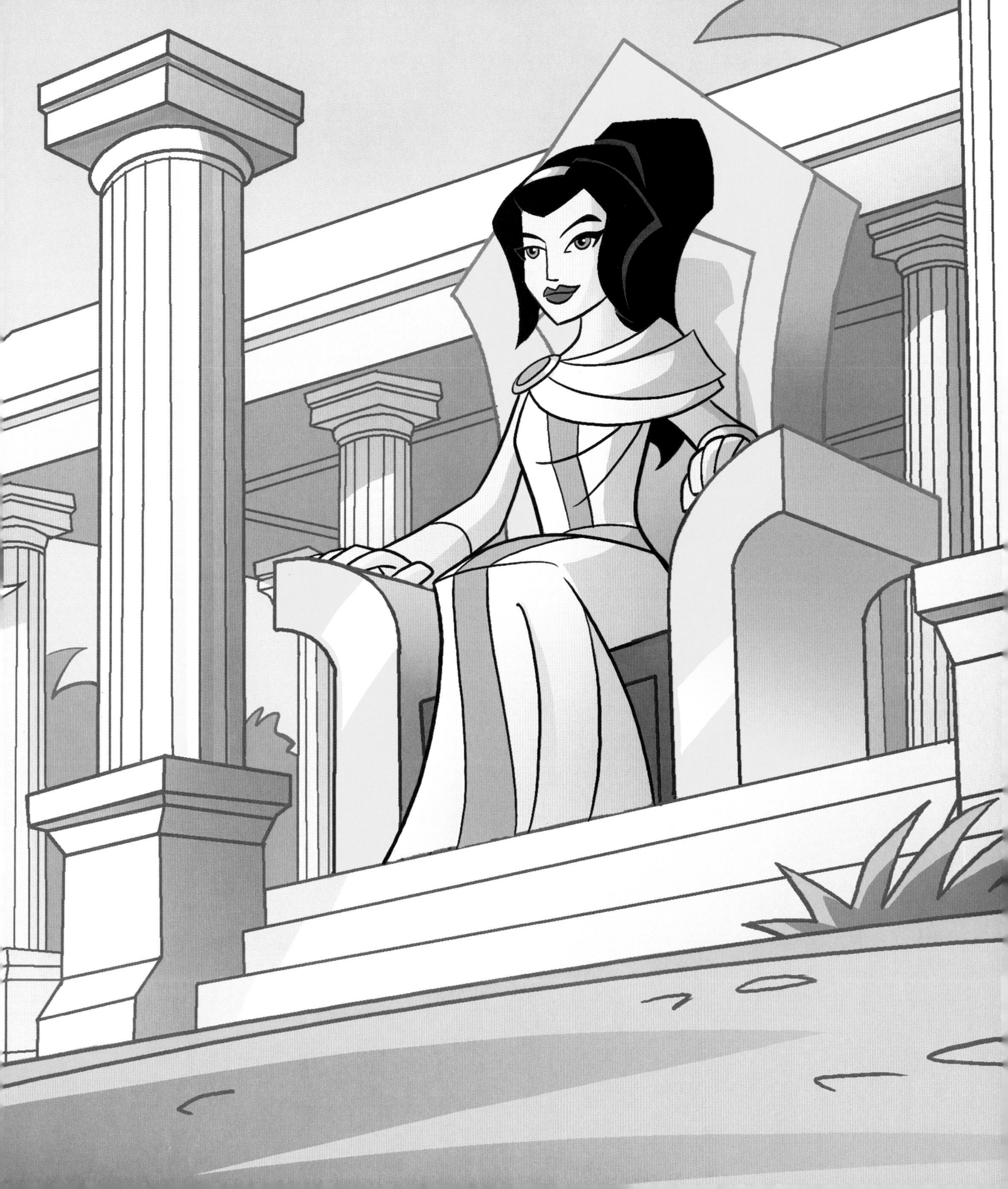

The Greek gods and goddesses gave Wonder Woman special powers to fight villains and evildoers everywhere.

Along with her physical gifts, she was given **wisdom** and **courage** to make smart decisions.

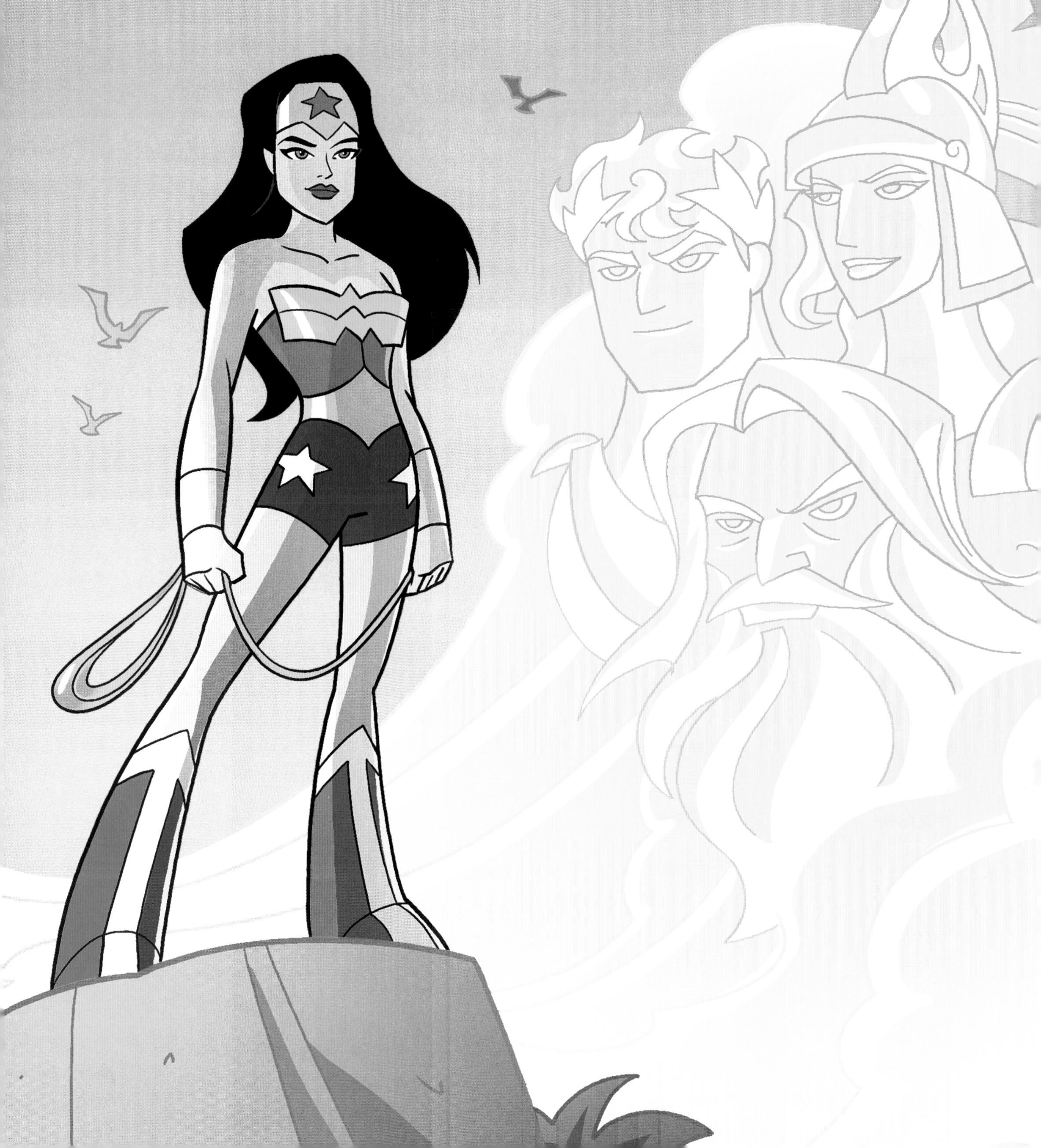

Wonder Woman can ***lift*** heavy objects, such as cars, trucks, and boats.

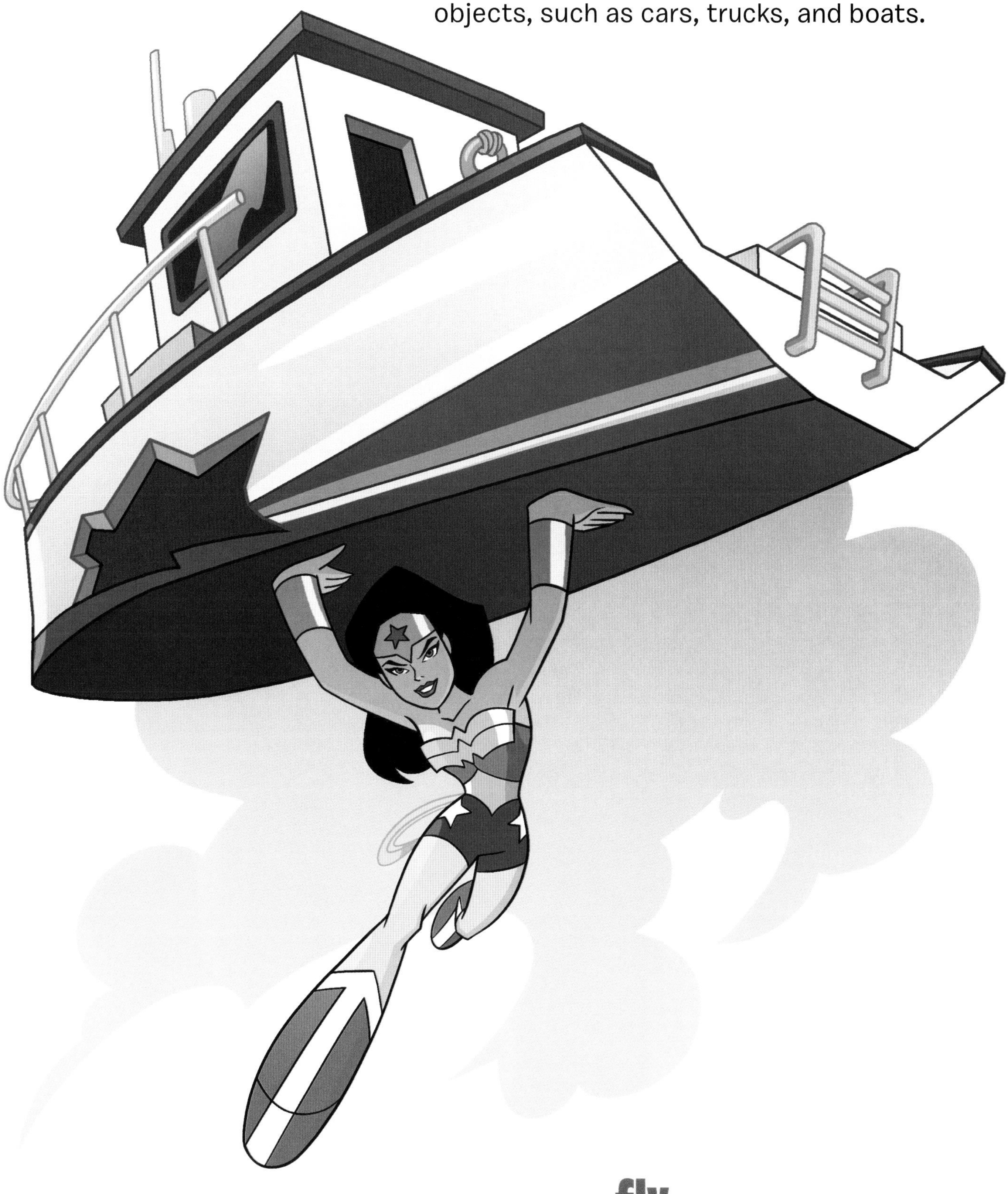

She can run faster than a train and **fly** through the air like a rocket! But her greatest strength is her passionate belief in protecting the innocent and fighting for justice.

Through many years of training, Wonder Woman perfected her Amazon warrior skills and became a master of **hand-to-hand combat**.

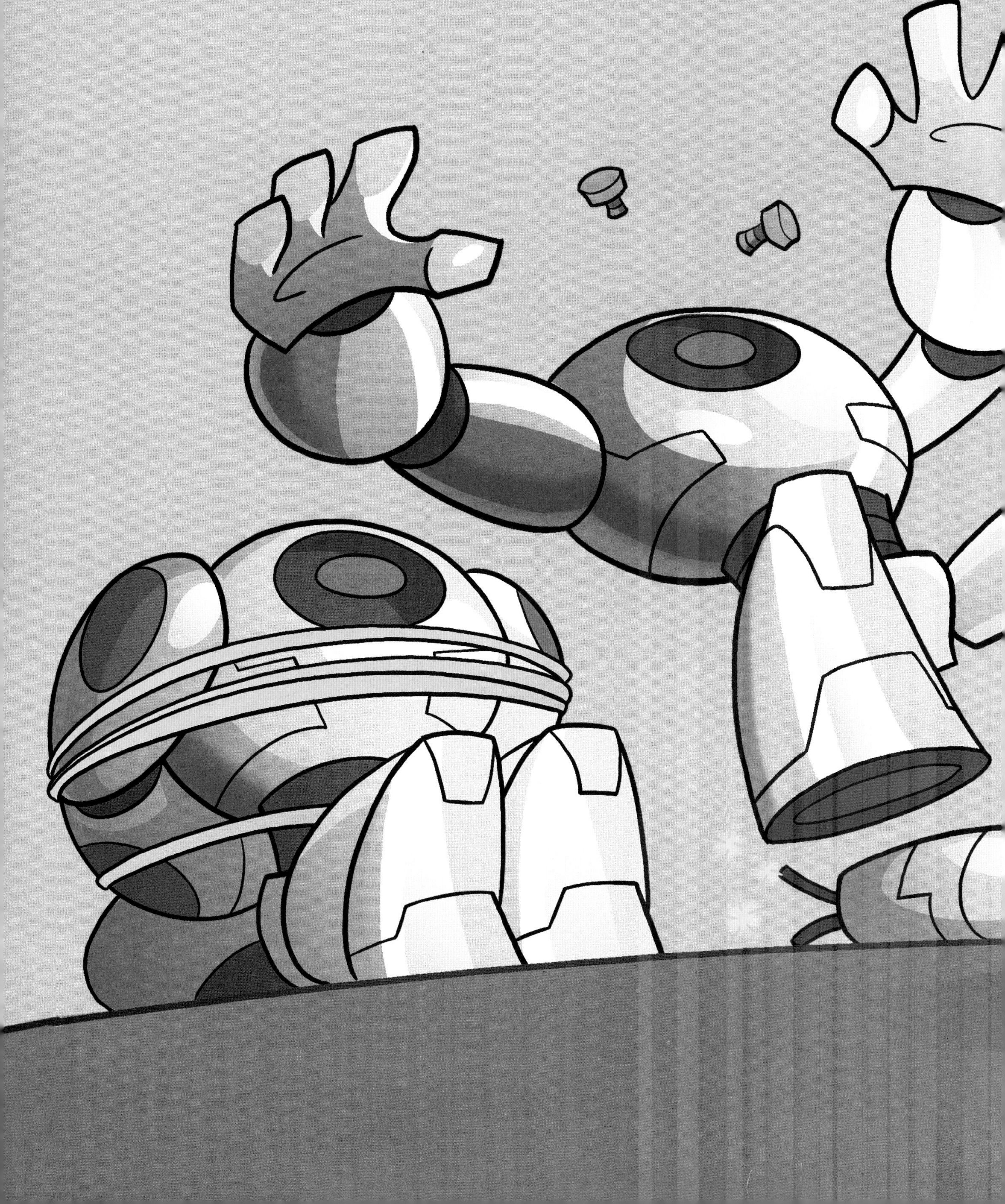

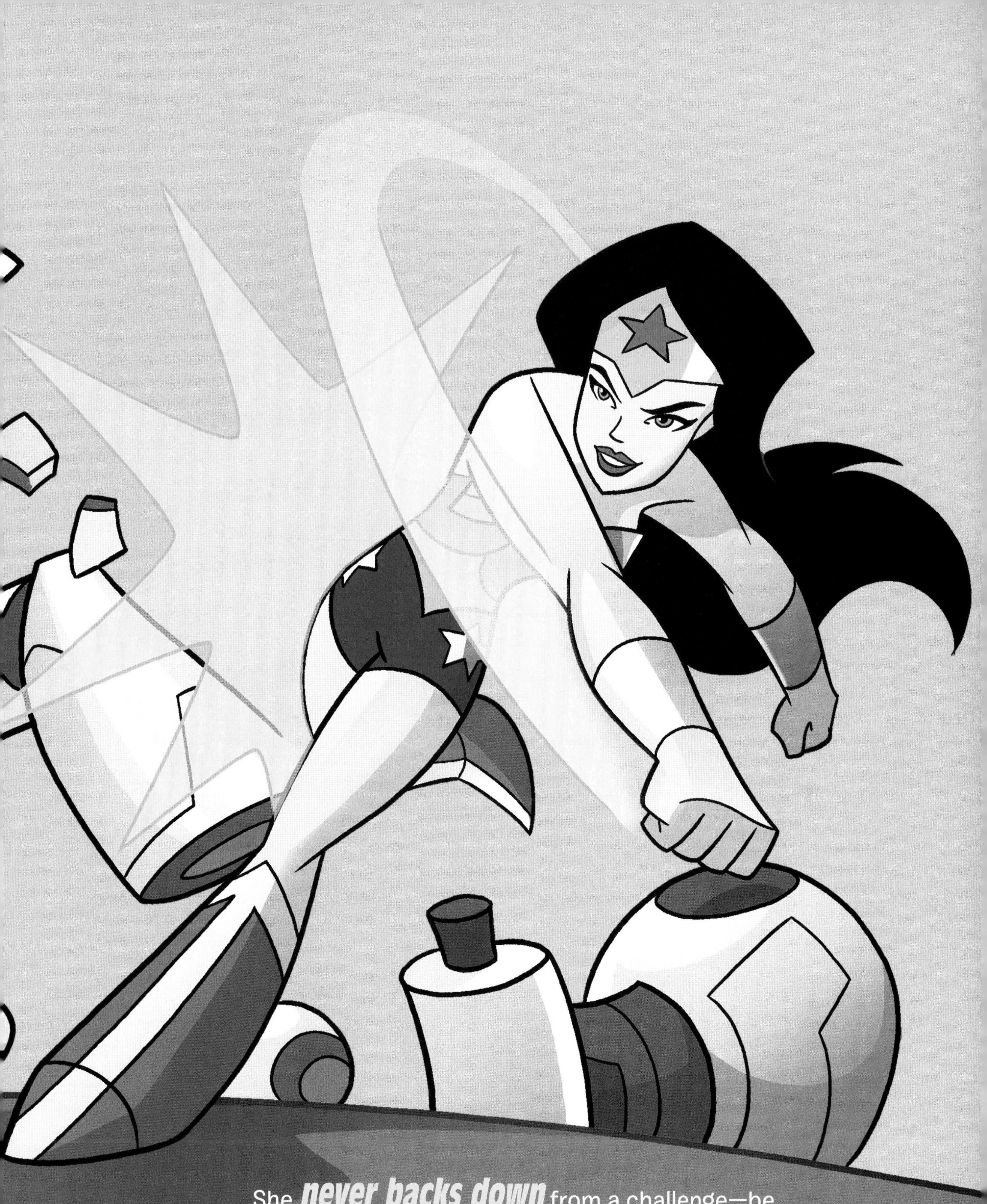

She ***never backs down*** from a challenge—be it facing Earth's mightiest super-villains or fending off an invasion of indestructible alien robots.

In battle, Wonder Woman has a number of **weapons** by her side. Her golden **tiara** becomes a boomerang that she can hurl at her enemies.

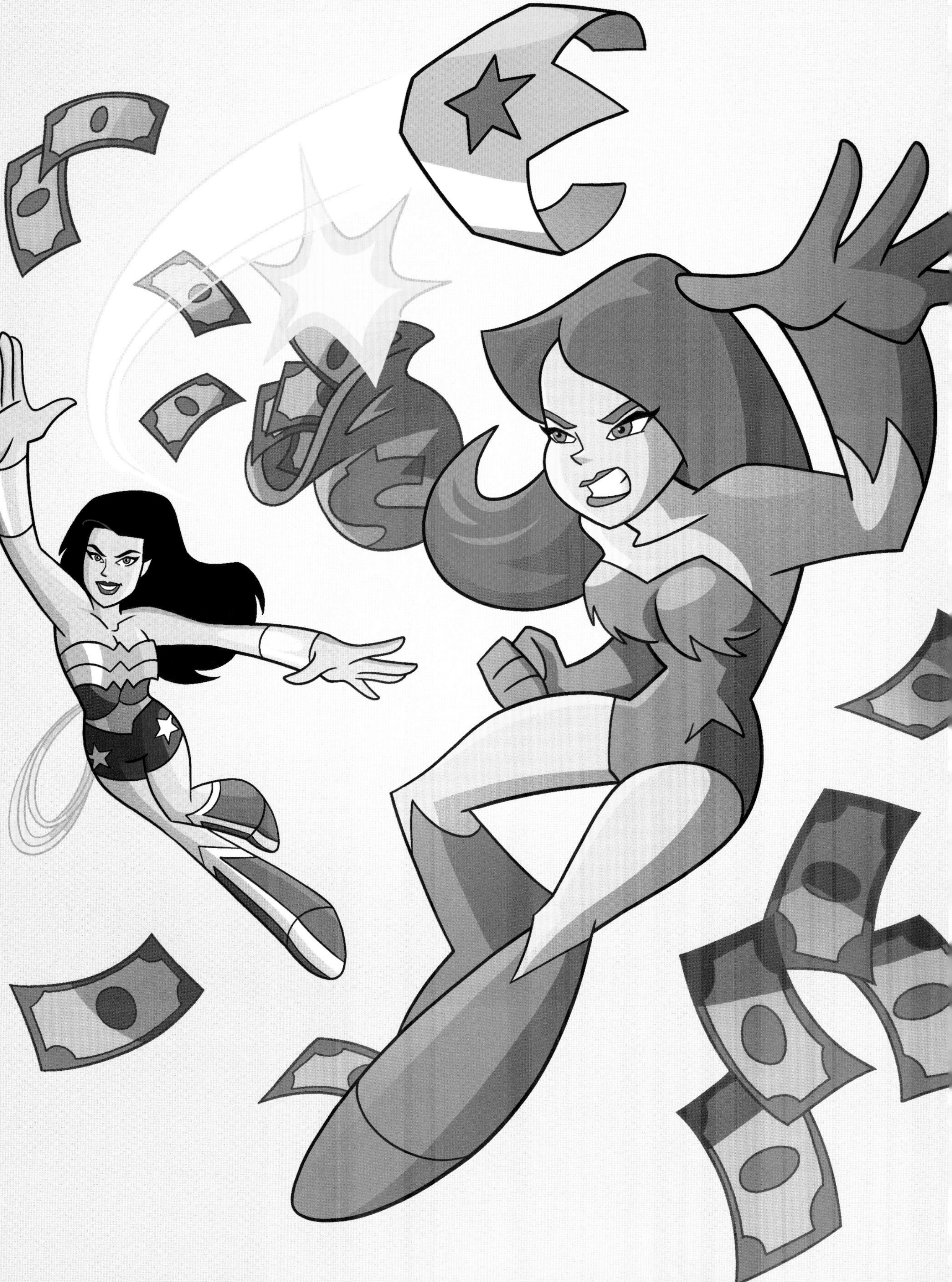

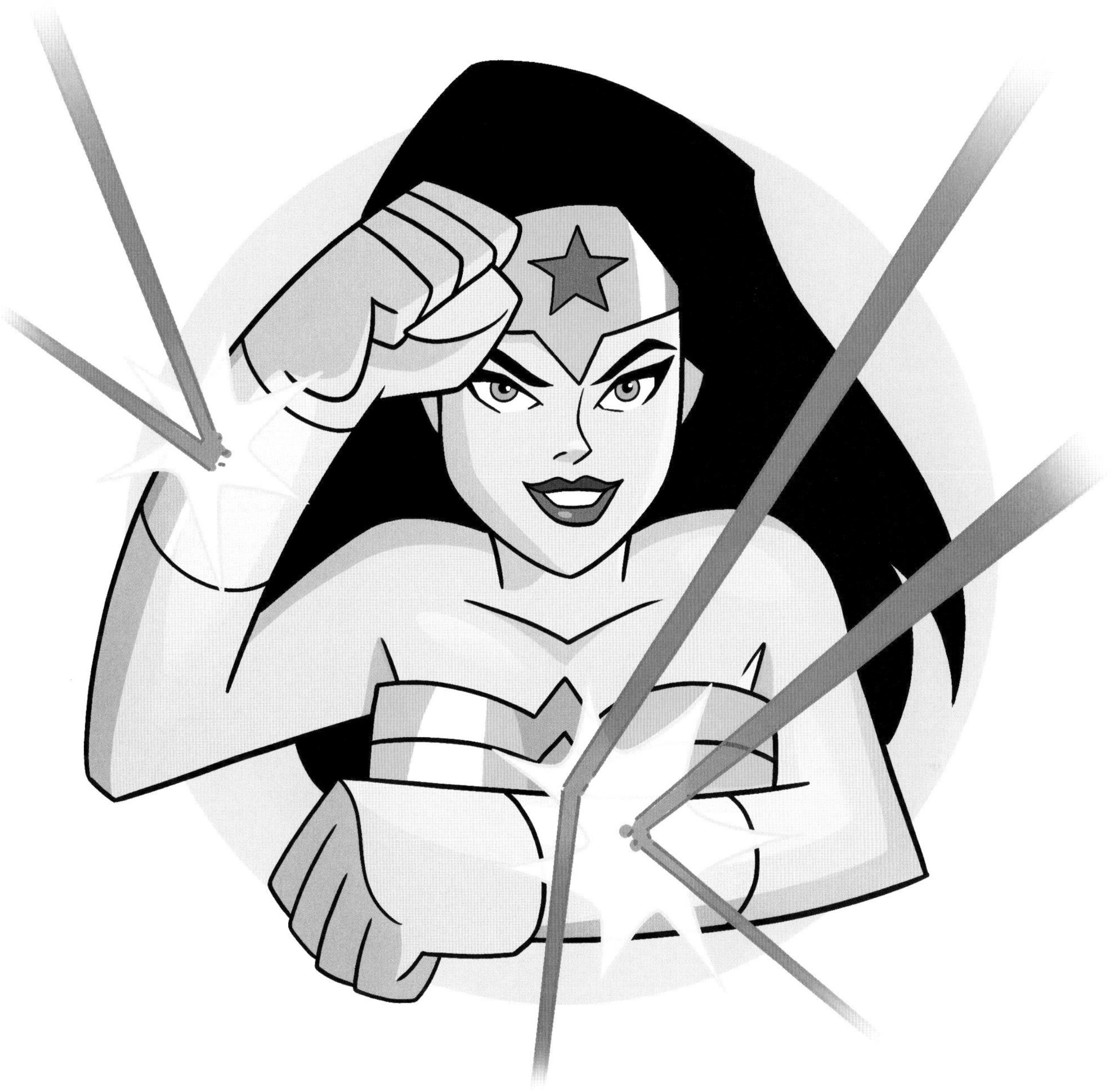

Wonder Woman's **bracelets** are indestructible. Her silver cuffs can ***deflect*** arrows, lasers, and even bolts of electricity!

Wonder Woman also has an **Invisible Jet** for rescues.

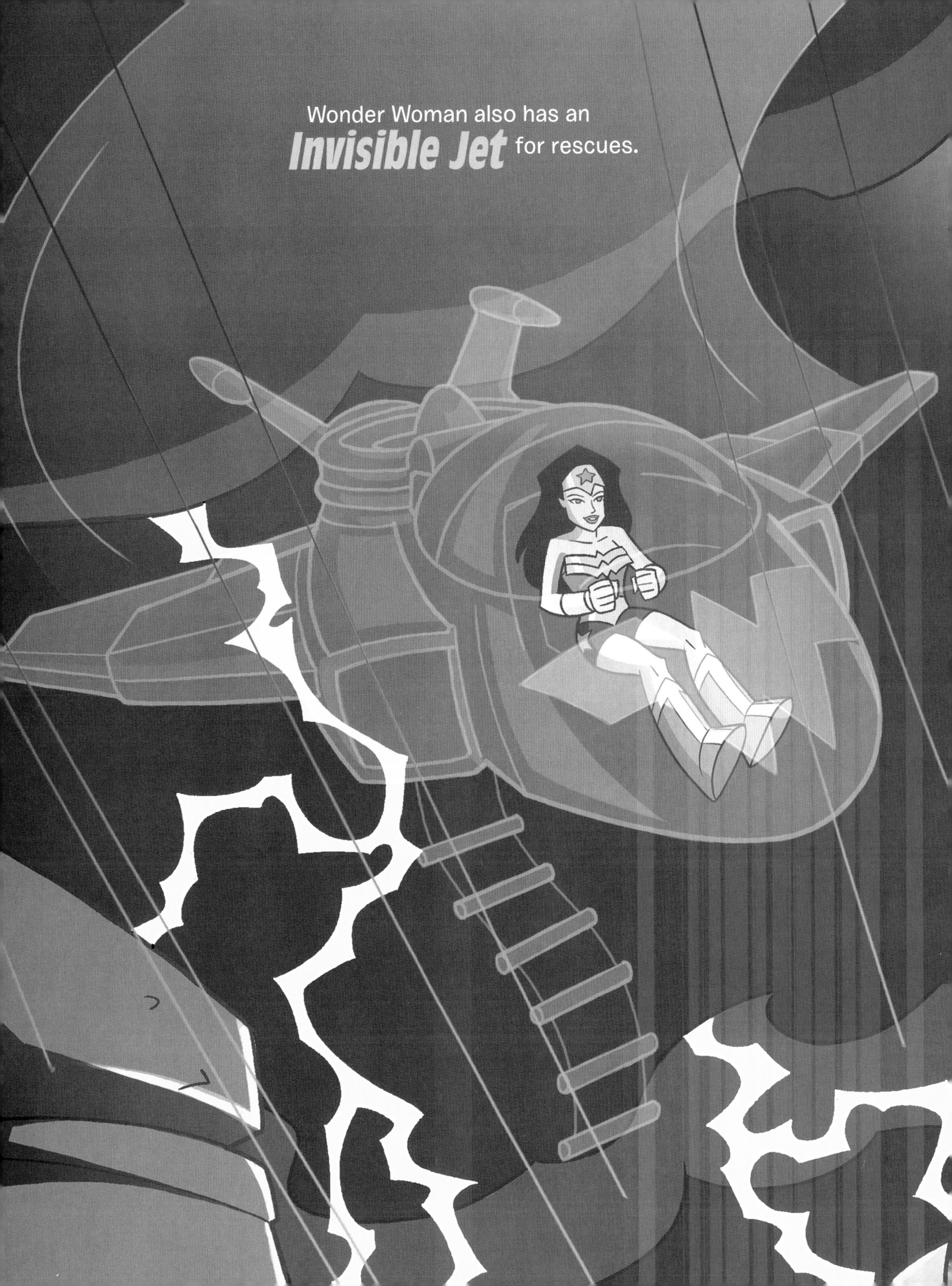

With its ultra-powerful engines, her jet can reach **supersonic** speeds and fly through all types of weather.

Wonder Woman's jet is completely silent and undetectable by radar, so it's perfect for **secret missions**!

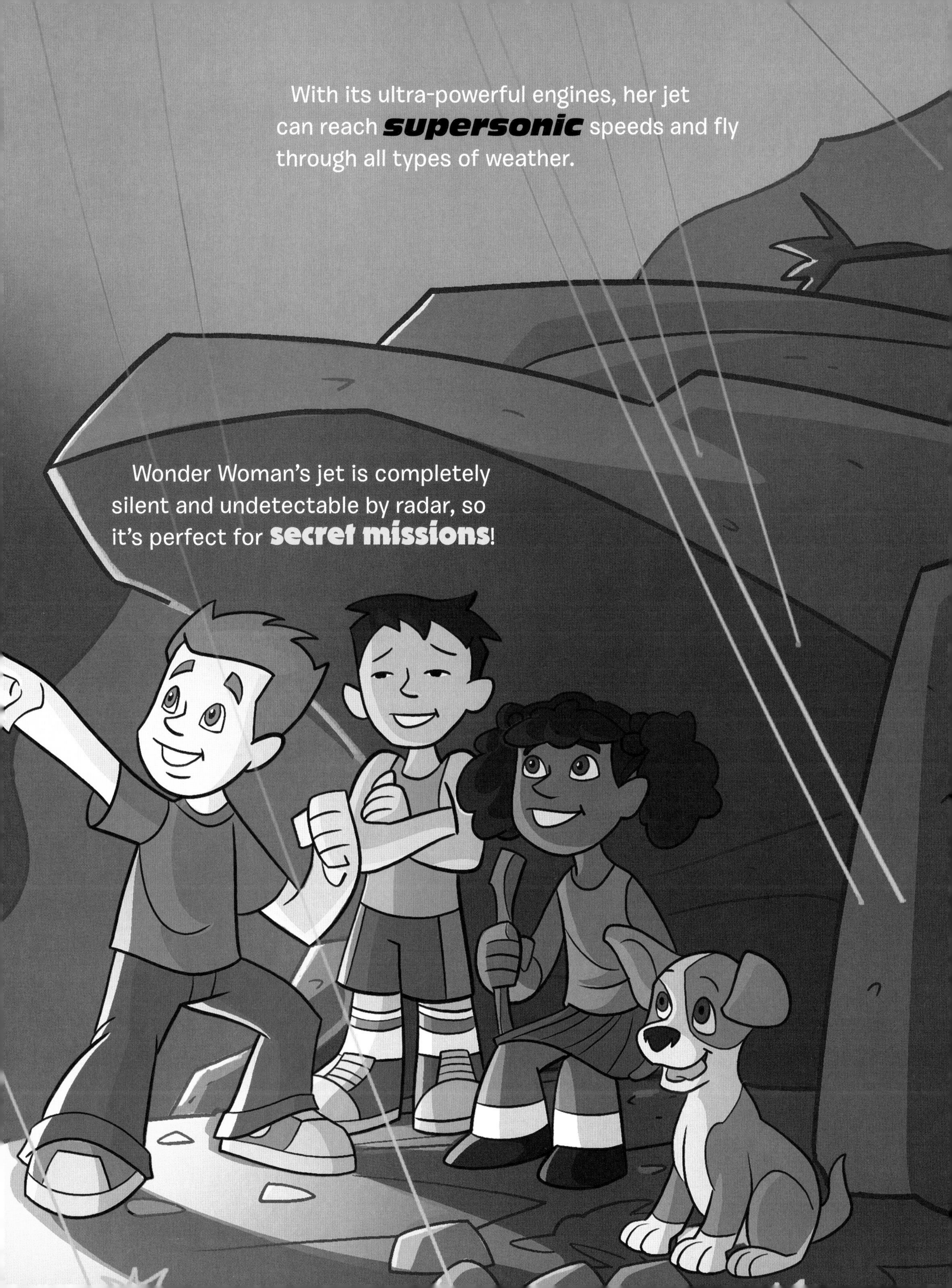

When Wonder Woman unleashes her ***Lasso of Truth***, villains have no choice but to tell the truth and confess their evil plans.

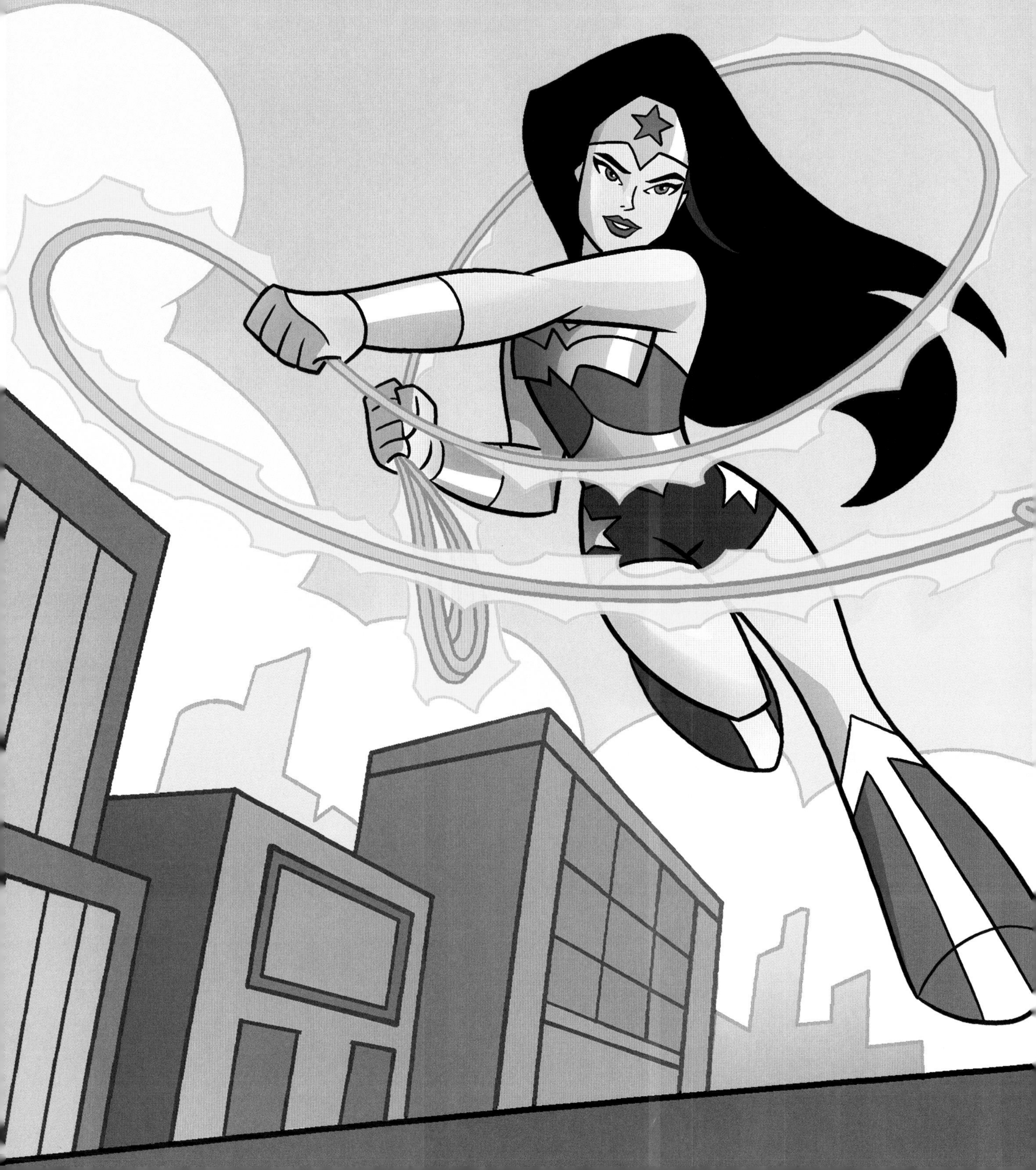

With its ability to stretch and shorten to any length, this **unbreakable** rope can be used to bind even the strongest villain.

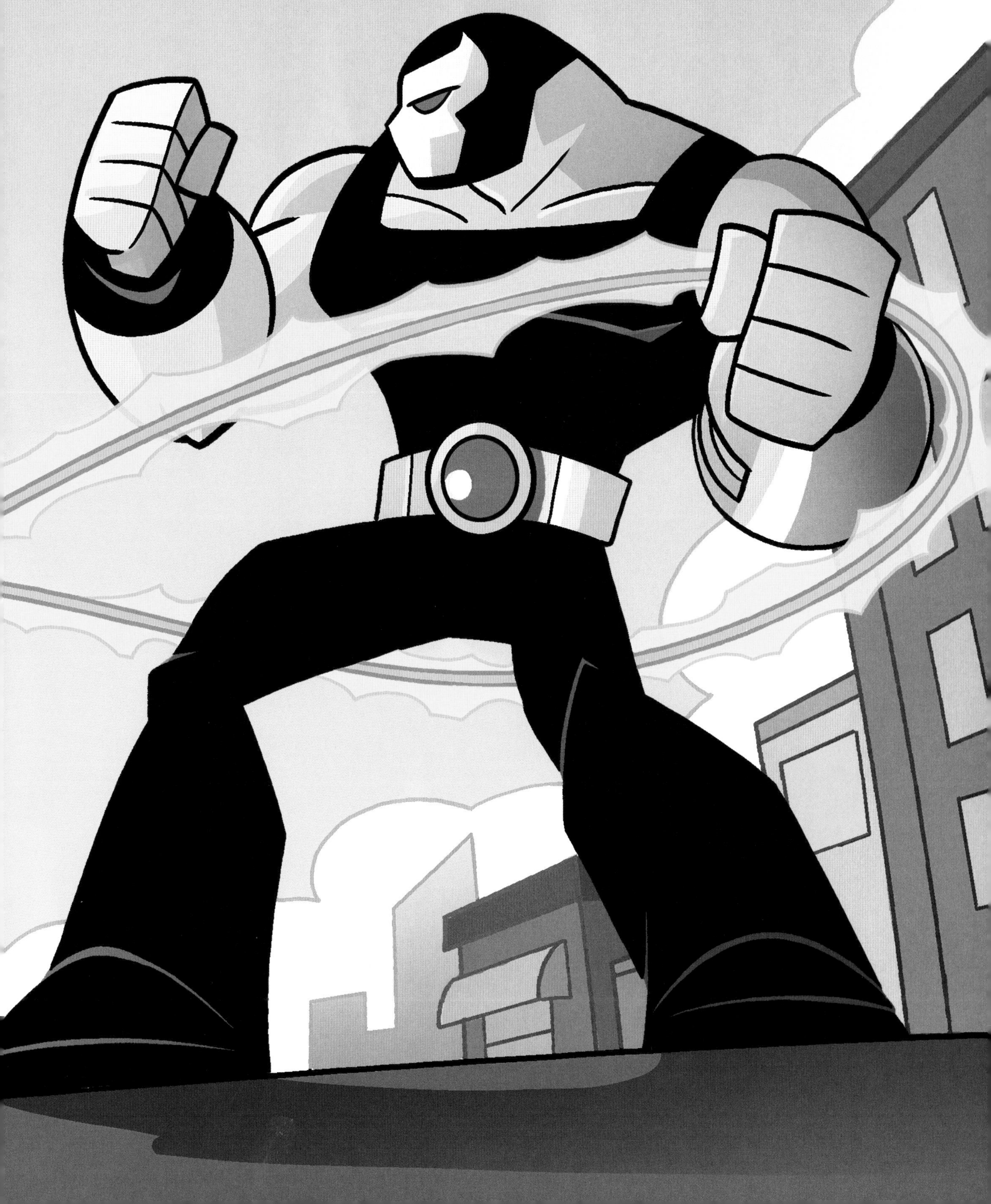

Wonder Woman has lots of enemies, but **Cheetah** is the most devious of them all. This fierce feline uses her razor-sharp teeth and destructive claws to commit all sorts of crimes!

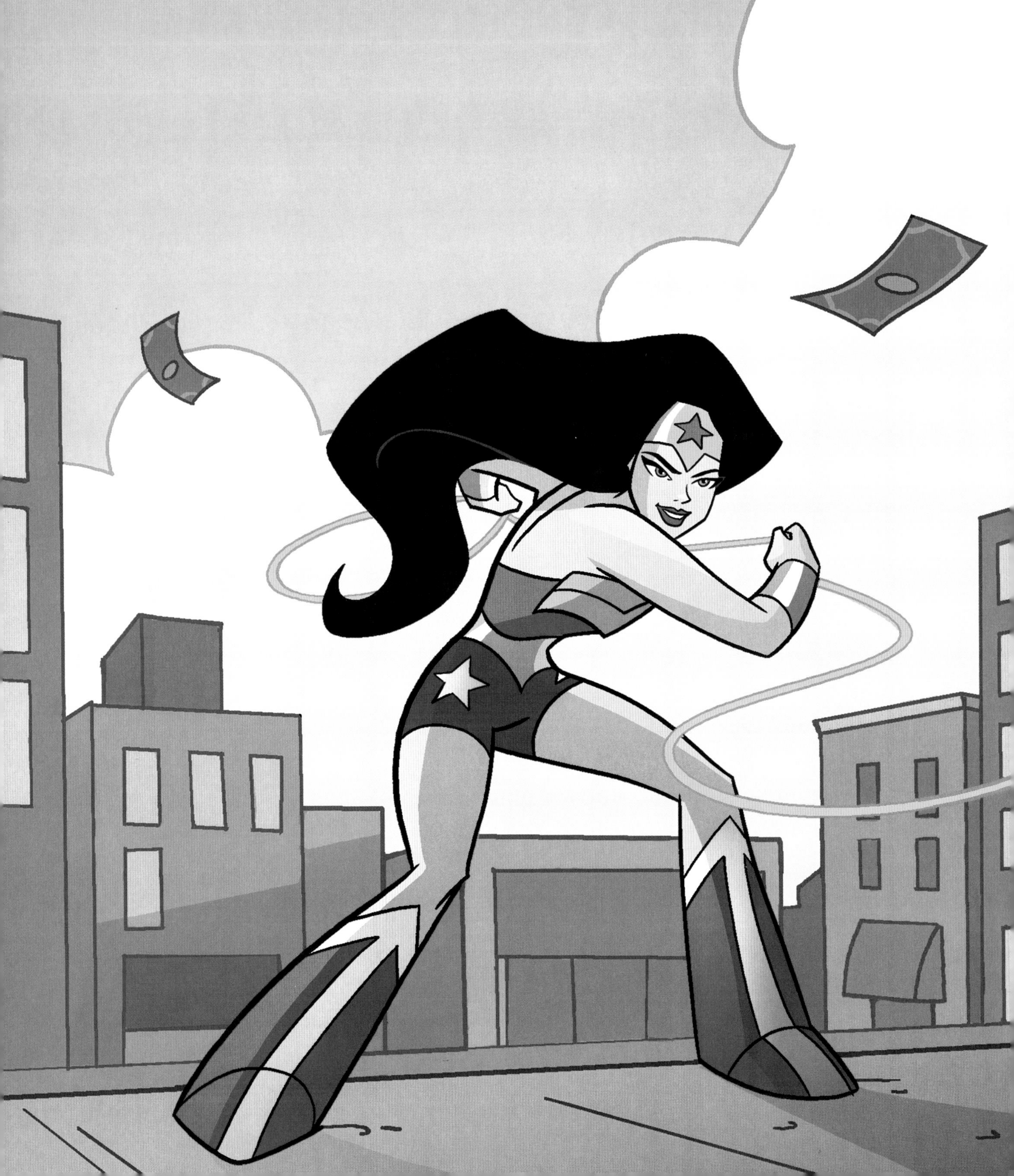

Cheetah and Wonder Woman have crossed paths many times. This crafty cat has tried to **swipe** Wonder Woman's Golden Lasso in hopes of making it her own. But Wonder Woman always stays one step ahead!

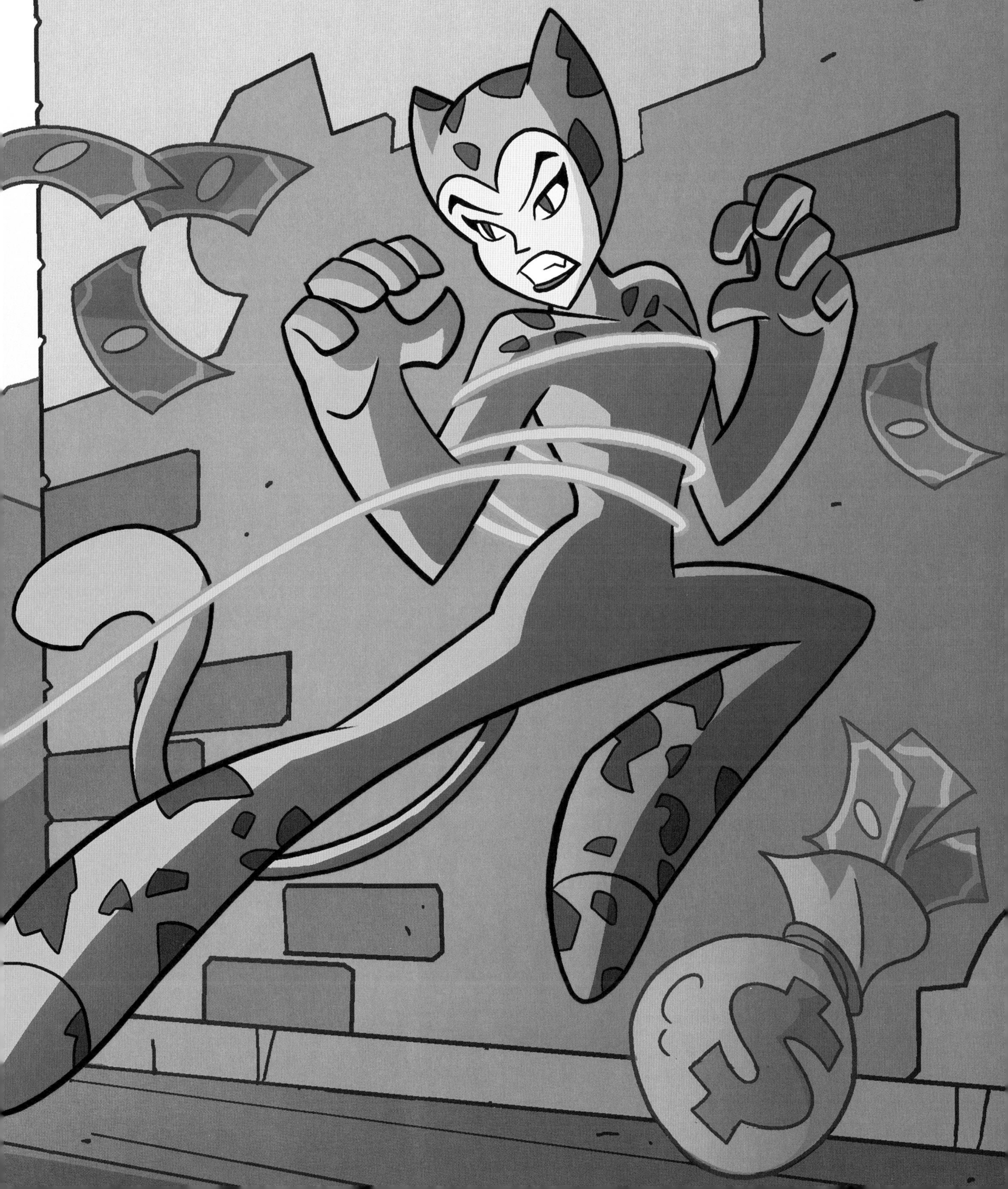

Wonder Woman is part of a team called the **Super Friends**. When Earth is threatened, these mighty heroes work together to keep the world safe! Each one brings special skills to the fight.

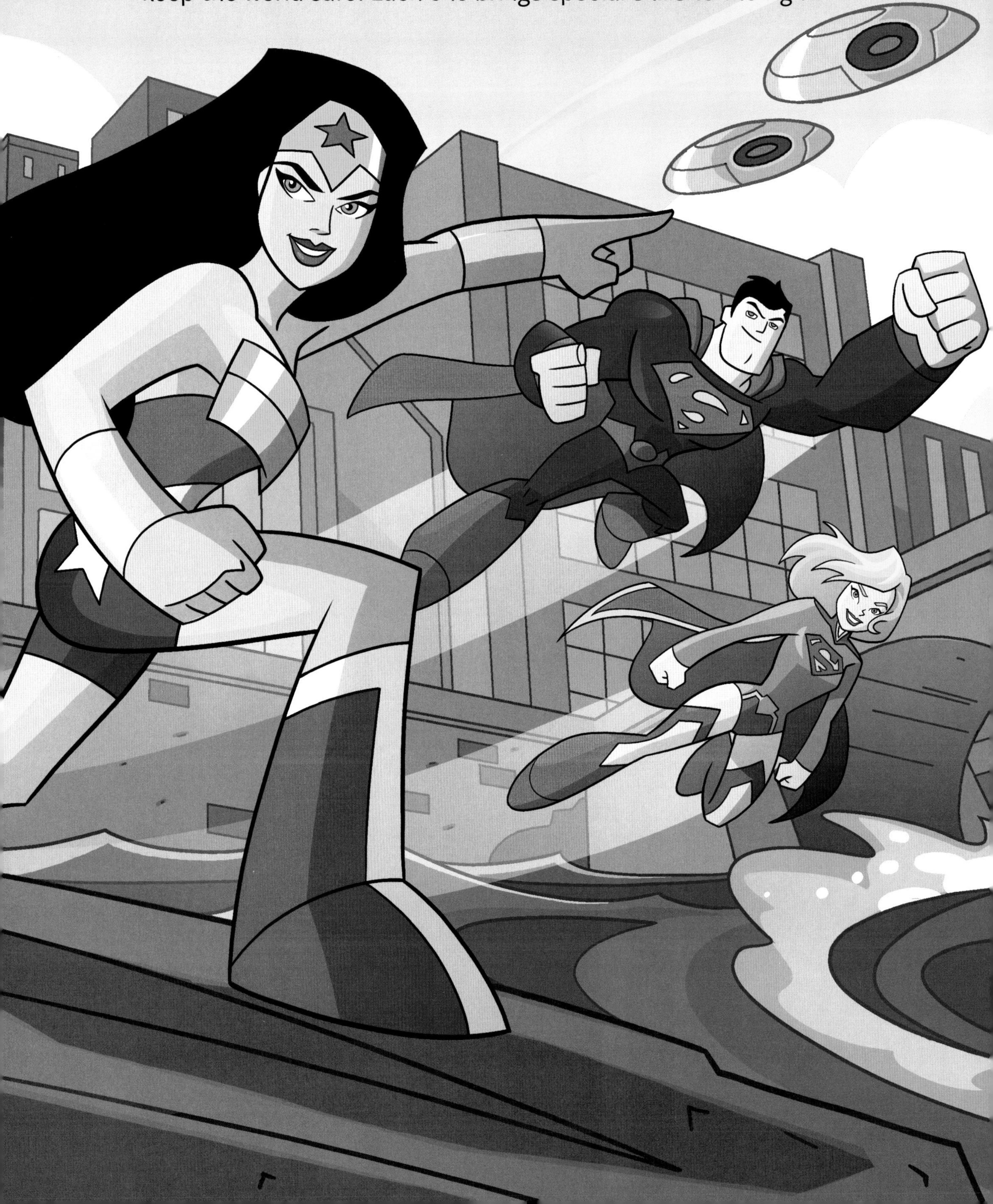

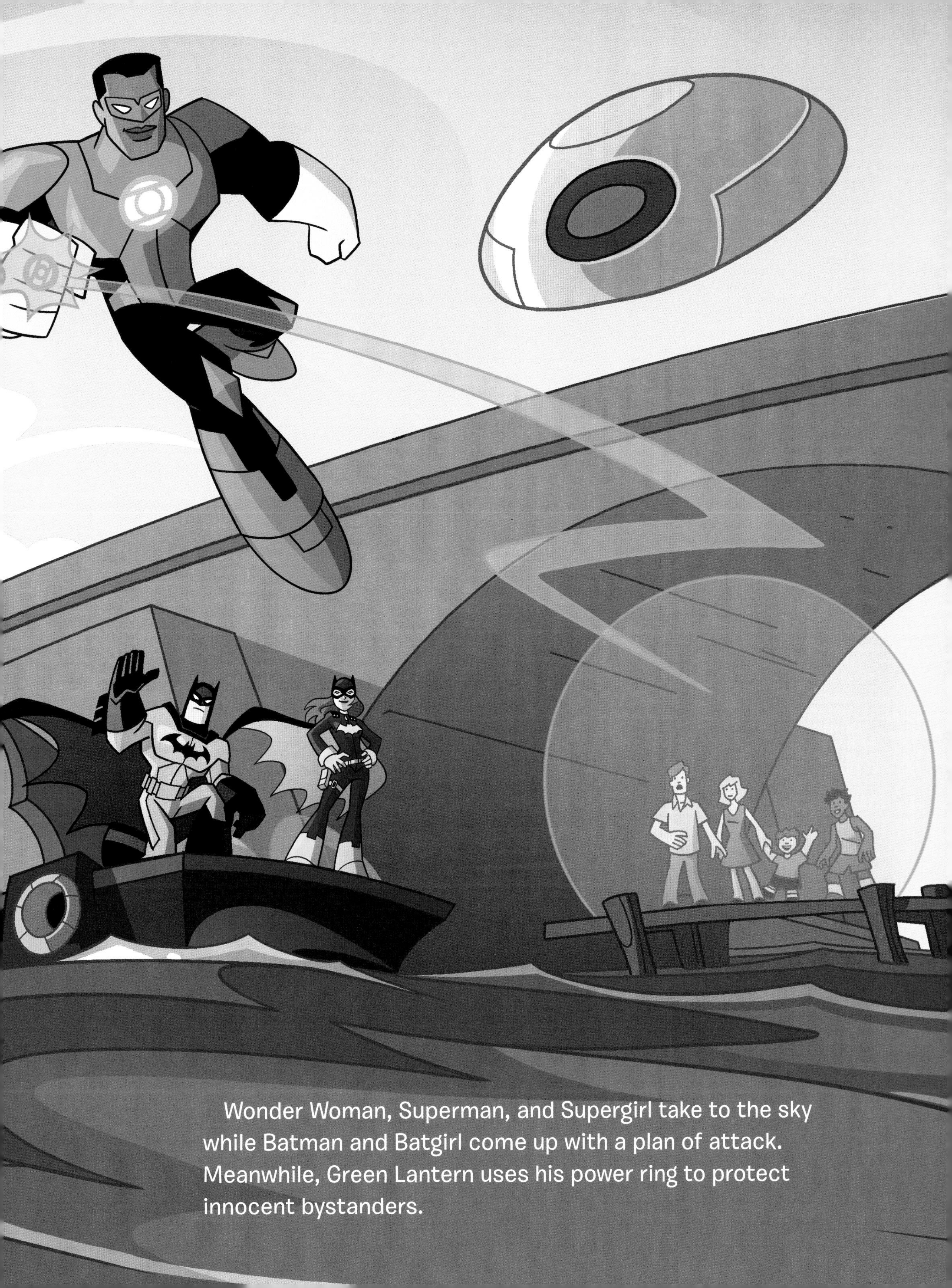

Wonder Woman, Superman, and Supergirl take to the sky while Batman and Batgirl come up with a plan of attack. Meanwhile, Green Lantern uses his power ring to protect innocent bystanders.

The heroes **swing into action!** First, Superman and Supergirl zip around the alien spaceships to confuse and distract the enemy. Then Green Lantern uses his magic ring to create defensive weapons and protective shields. Wonder Woman gets ready to use her super-strong bracelets to deflect alien energy beams, while Batman and Batgirl try to trip up the alien ships with their Batarangs and Batropes.

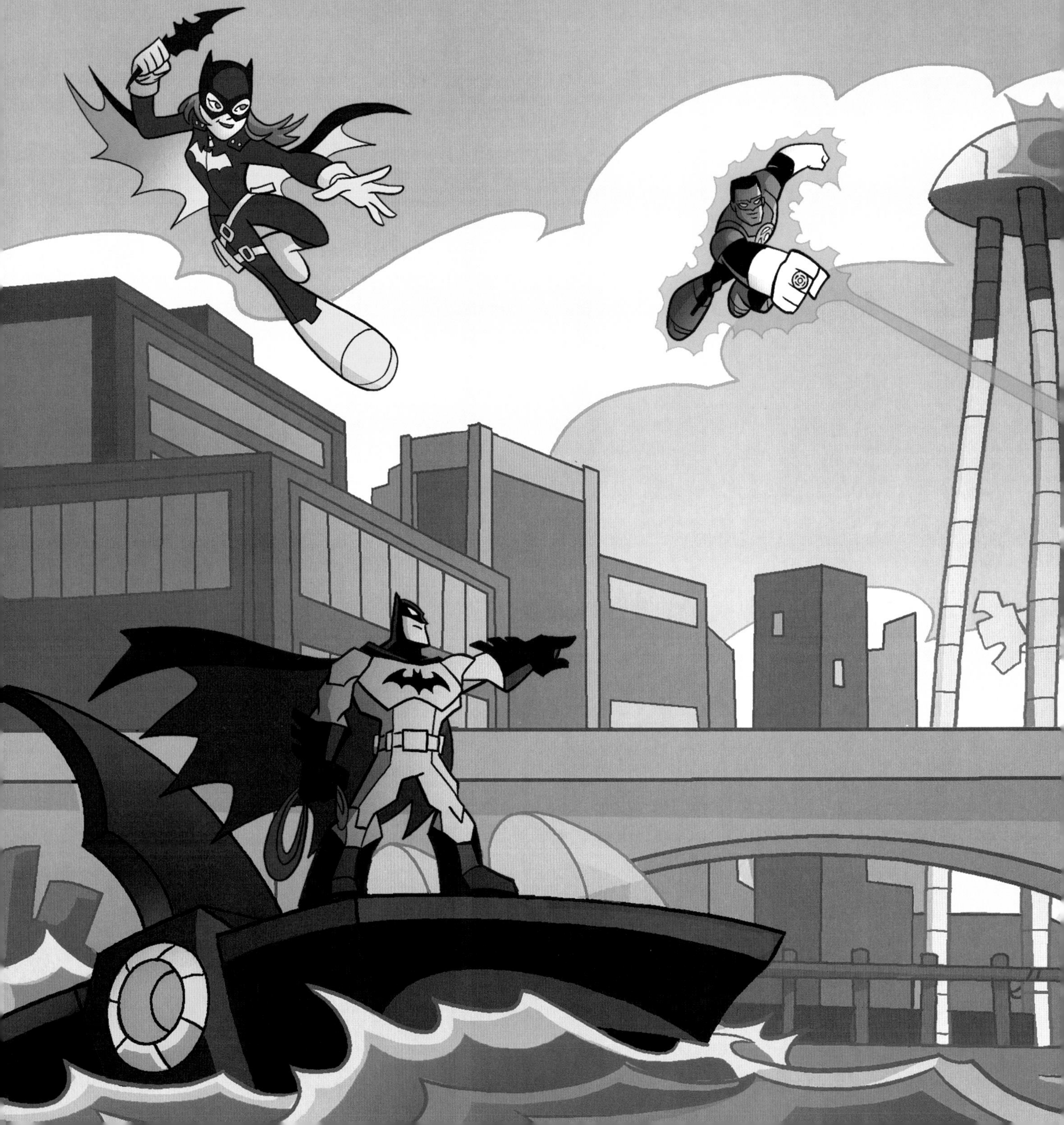

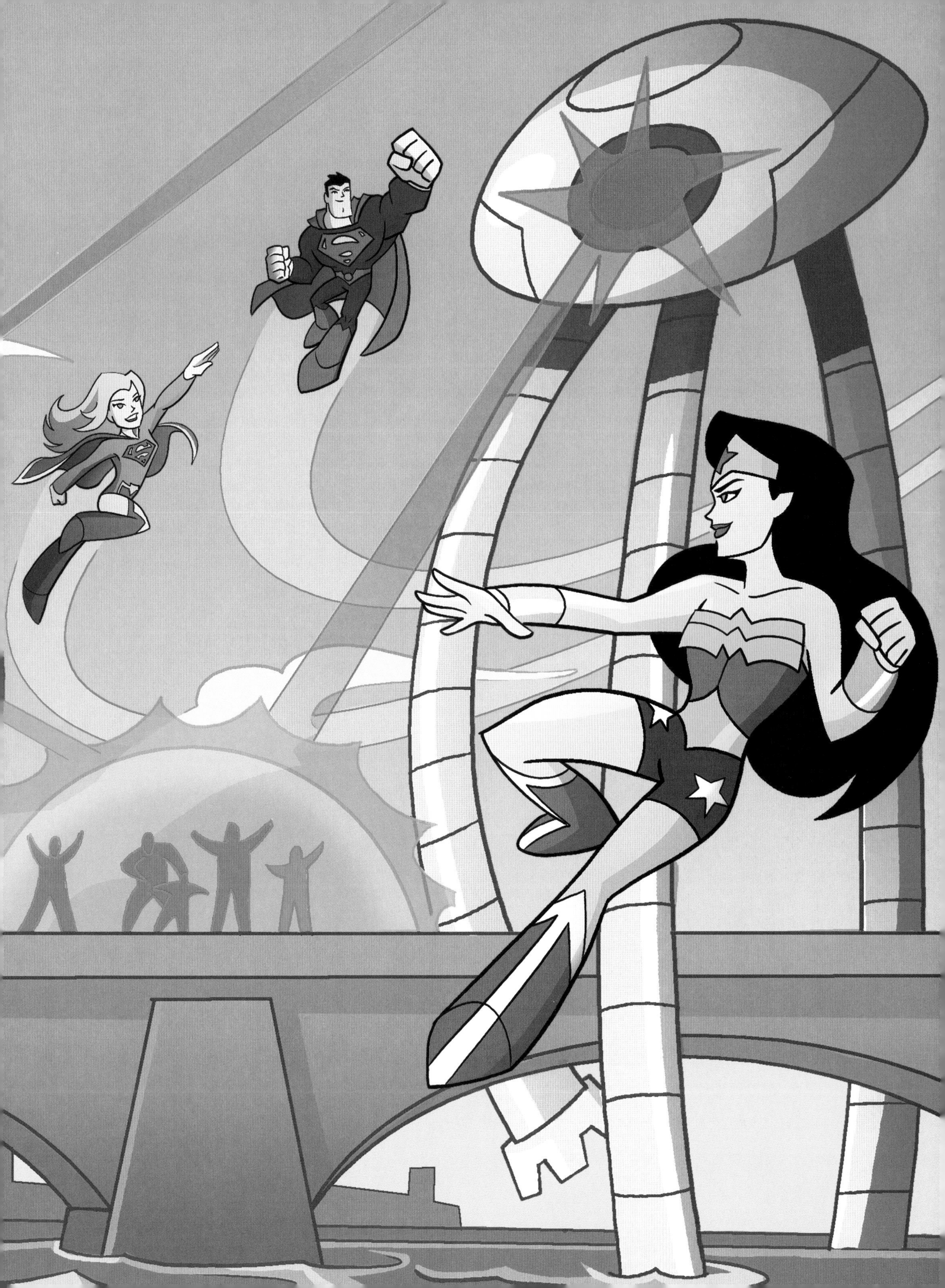

The Super Friends ***battle tirelessly*** to protect the world from harm. Using teamwork, they drive back alien invasions and capture many treacherous villains! No matter the threat, Wonder Woman never hesitates to join the battle to fight for what's right. She is proud to be a member of this ***amazing team of heroes!***

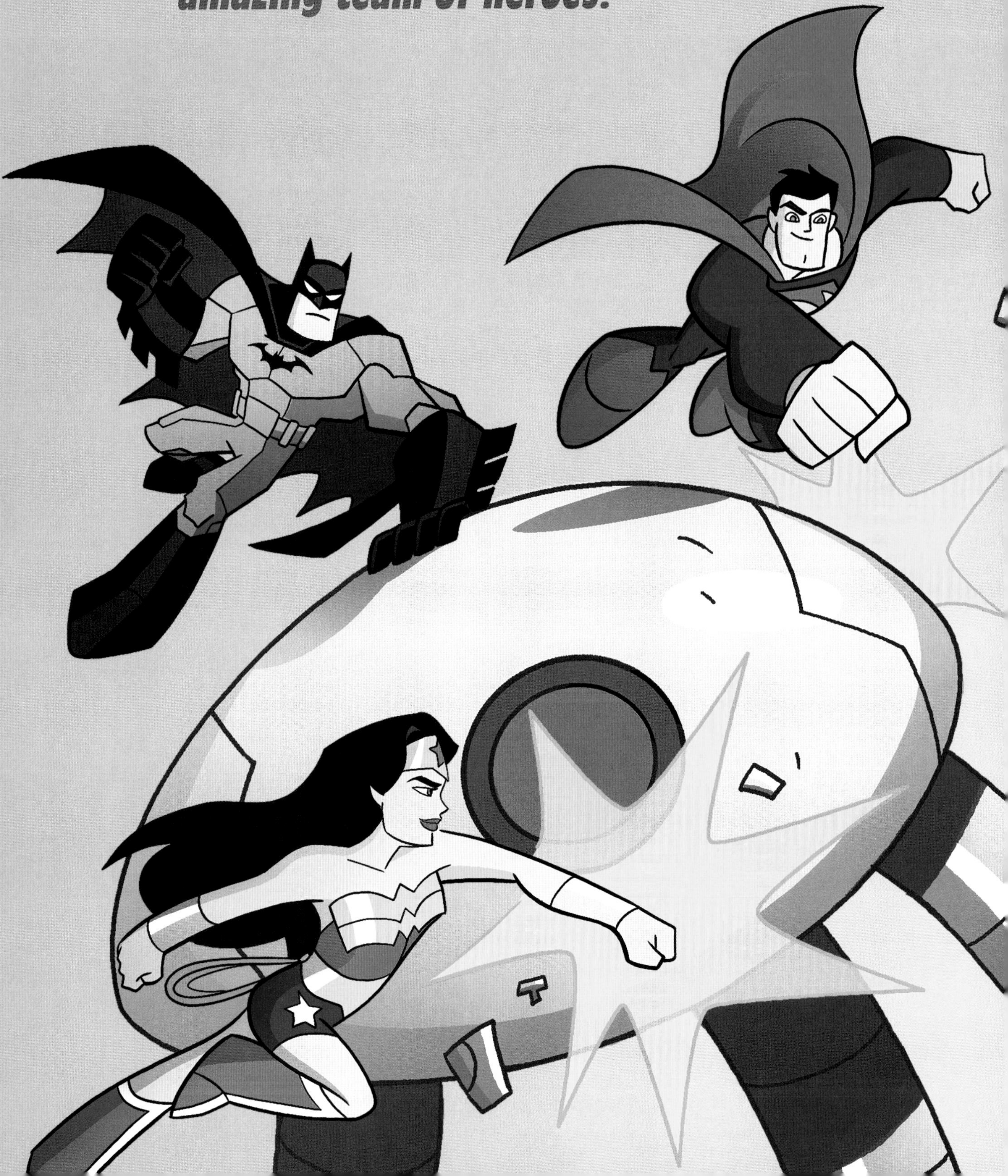

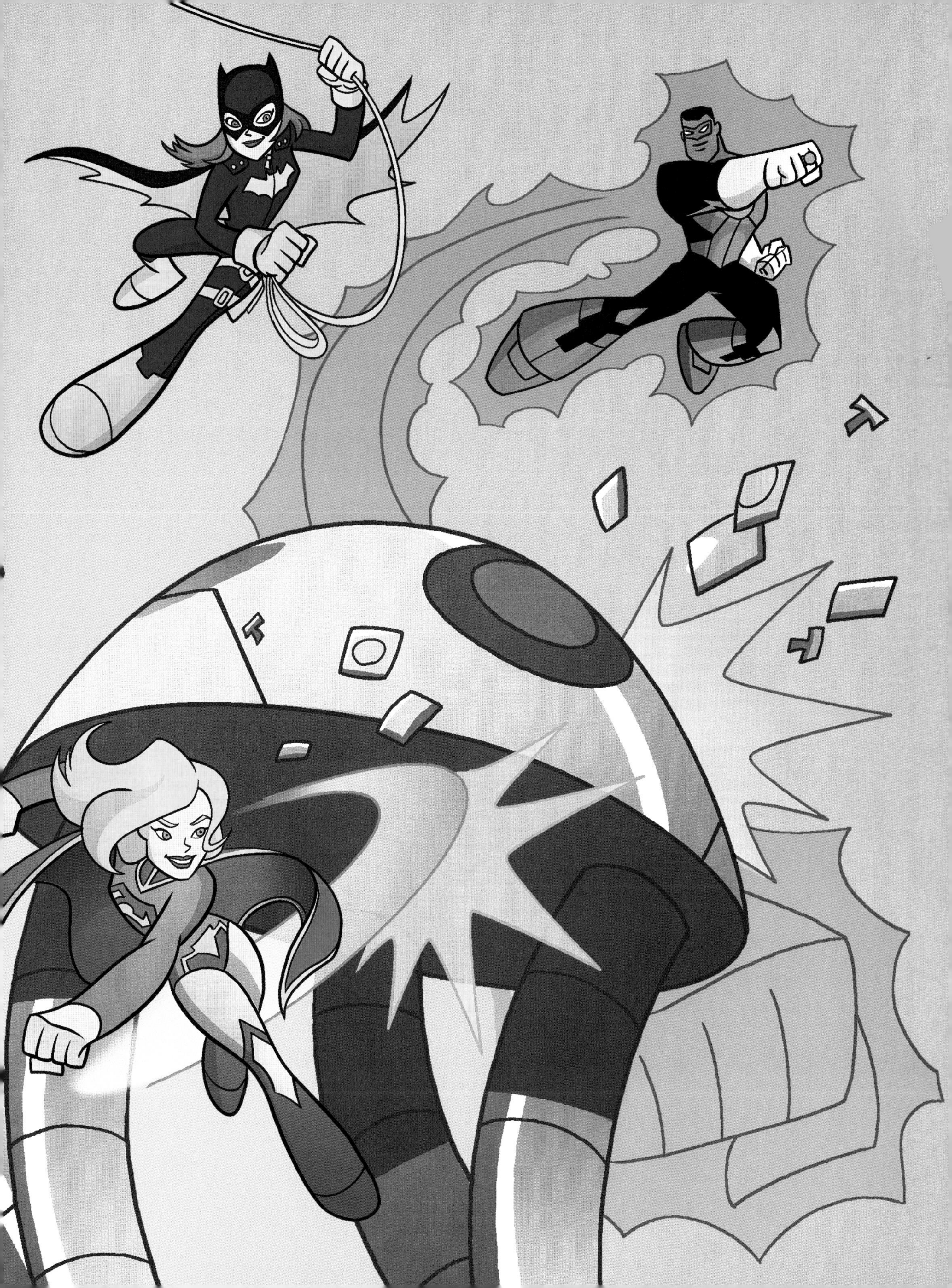

When the world needs a **wise**, **powerful**, and *brave hero*— it's Wonder Woman to the rescue!

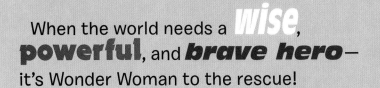